Teenage
Adventure Stories

Hannah C.E Lamont

To order additional copies of this book, contact:
Xlibris
UK TFN: 0800 0148620 (Toll Free inside the UK)
UK Local: 02036 956328 (+44 20 3695 6328 from outside the UK)
www.xlibrispublishing.co.uk
Orders@ Xlibrispublishing.co.uk

ISBN: Softcover   978-1-6641-1515-6
       EBook   978-1-6641-1516-3

Library of Congress Control Number: 2021905030

Print information available on the last page

Rev. date: 03/18/2021

Table of Contents

The Unicorn Keeper

Once long ago, a beautiful young woman called Summer and her father lived in a small cottage in Scotland. She was very smart and loved to read. Summer also had a good friend named Tony.

Sometime ago Summer was hurt in an accident which left her scarred. Though she grew up sweet, kind, and lovely, she was sad and lonely. She grew up in a small village, and some of the villagers were mean to her. But Summer didn't care as she had her friend Tony to talk to. Or so she thought. But when she tried to speak to him now, he did not pay attention to her anymore.

Hurt and heartbroken, Summer felt that she had no one to talk to anymore. So she decided to leave. When night fell, she kissed her beloved father on the head and off she went.

Summer took a boat far away into the Highlands. After she got off the boat, she walked for hours, until she could walk no more. She found a quiet little cave, where she lay down and fell asleep.

When Summer awoke, she was surrounded by unicorns! But she was not scared because she knew quite a lot about unicorns from her books. So she decided to get to know them. Even learn how to speak their language.

After a few days passed, Summer was outside watching the unicorns when she heard the noise of someone approaching her. When she turned around, Summer saw a woman standing there. She introduced herself to Summer as June. June explained that she had been watching over Summer and noticed how kind and sweet she was with the unicorns, and she must have known a lot about unicorns. June knew Summer was hungry, so she invited to her cottage to wash up and have some food, and offered her a place to stay.

As they went to the lake, Summer asked June who the beautiful girl was in the lake. June replied, 'Why that is you, Summer.'

Summer looked confused. June explained, 'It is a magic lake. It shows a person's heart and soul inside instead of outside.'

June left Summer to get washed and put on new clothes for dinner. As they sat down to eat, June asked Summer to tell her about herself. After Summer told her everything that happened, June knew she was not ready to go home. So she asked her to stay and look after and protect the unicorns while she went on errands. Summer agreed, and she became the unicorn keeper!

Summer felt a nice bond with June, and it felt strange to her. It was like she had known known June her whole life. And they both knew that they were going to be very good friends and that June would never hurt Summer.

One day after a long day's work, Summer decided to sit by the lake. All of a sudden, two strangers appeared. They were lost and confused. They did not know where they were. They walked over to Summer and asked her for help. As she turned around to talk to them, they saw her injured face. But they did not run away. They did not even seem to be afraid. Instead, they just introduced themselves. Their names were Jay and Lex. 'My name is Summer,' she introduced herself.

Suddenly, June came running towards her. She looked scared. 'What's wrong?' Summer asked.

'The unicorns are in danger. An evil woman named Snegurochka, which means snow maiden, wants to keep the unicorns for herself so she will be more powerful,' June explained.

Summer looked and felt sad. June asked her what was wrong.

Summer told her, 'It is not right for them to be chased out of their homes. I know what that is like. We should fight for their right to stay in where they are safe.' Lex and Jay said that they would be more than happy to help if they needed them. Summer introduced them to June, and she agreed that it was a good idea, and more help would be good.

They packed some food and water and off they went on their journey to help the unicorns. It was going to be a long and hard journey, so they decided to set up camp for the night. Summer could not sleep, so she went for a walk and sat by a tree near a lake. She heard someone come up behind her. It was Lex. He asked if everything was okay. She replied, 'Yes, just getting some water for the journey tomorrow.' He mention how great June and Jay were getting on great. She agreed.

As Summer was about to walk away when Lex said that he would like for them to get to know each other like Jay and June were. She asked what he meant, but she thought she kind of knew. Still, she was scared about getting hurt. But something inside her said, *It's okay.*

Summer told him everything about herself. Then she asked Lex to tell her about himself. After they talked, Summer and Lex found that they had so much in common. As it was getting late and they had to get up early, they said goodnight to each other.

The next morning, Summer, Lex, June, and Jay got up and ready for the other part of their journey. They had not far to go. Lex and Jay asked the girls what the plan was. Summer told him that the best and safe way was to try to talk to Snegarochka and make her see a different point of view. Lex asked, 'But what if that doesn't work?' When Summer, looking confused, asked what he meant, Lex said, 'We might need to fight.'

Getting a wee bit annoyed, Summer said, 'It won't come to that. Based on what June and I know, she is hurting inside. She thinks owning a unicorn will bring her beauty. So we have to show her that's not the case,' and she walked off. June explained to Lex that Summer was in the same position as Snegurochka.

After June explained and after he considered what Summer told him the night before, Lex went up to Summer and told her that he understood and everything would be fine. And he told Summer how sweet and kind and beautiful she was. She thanked him, and he laid a gentle kiss on her lips.

Lex and Summer rejoined the group, and they all continued to their destination. They went inside the tattered old cottage they went inside and then out the back door and saw Snegurochka. Summer had a strange feeling towards her. It was like she knew her. Snegurochka asked who they were, and June said she and Summer looked after the unicorns.

When Snegurochka asked if they brought her one, Summer said, 'No. They don't belong to anyone. We just look after them so no harm comes to them.'

But Snegurochka said that she needs one to be beautiful again. She had been in an accident a long time ago, and she needed to be how she looked before so she could get back to her family.

Then Summer said, 'I understand everything. I was in an accident too. I ran away, and June, who is now my best friend, took me in. June is very kind and gentle. And see, we met some other people on the way. It turns out that you don't need to look beautiful to be beautiful. As long as you're kind and gentle and have people who love you, then you'll be okay.'

Snegurochka said that Summer was right, and she was sorry that she had been so much trouble. She asked what their names were, and they introduced themselves. 'And my name is Summer,' she responded last.

Snegurochka looked surprised. 'Summer, is that you?'

'Yes, do I know you?' Summer replied.

Snegurochka said, 'I'm your mother.' Summer ran up to her and hugged her, and asked how she came to be up here. Snegurochka explained, 'When the fire broke out, I was scared you and your dad must have thought that I didn't make it. I was going to look for you and then I stopped for some water. That's when I saw my face, so I ran away. A few years later I heard about a herd of unicorns, and well you know the rest.'

Summer explained how much she and her dad missed her. And with that, they made their way home.

Summer and her mum went back to her dad's house and gave him a big surprise. They both started telling him about the adventure they had.

Summer's mum and dad lived in their little cottage. As for Summer, June, Jay, and Lex, they all stayed up the Highlands to look after the unicorns. And in case you didn't know, they all got married and lived happily ever after.

A Mysterious Royal Tale

Once upon a time there was a maid called Mia who worked for the king and queen and their daughter, Roseita, The royal family was very kind to Mia as her mother was very good friends with the king and queen. But sadly, Mia's mother passed on to the angels, so Mia worked in the castle.

Roseita learned her royal duties, but that never stopped them from being good friends. One day after Mia's chores and

Roseita's duties were finished, they decided to play their usual game. They played dress up, each putting on the other's clothes. Then they went out to the palace garden and had a walkabout.

The girls played and laughed until the came to a drawbridge. As they were walking across it, two crocodiles suddenly came up and tried to bite Mia. A boy was riding by the palace, and he heard someone screaming. So he rode to see what was wrong. When he got there, he saw the frightened girls. He rode towards them and scared the crocodiles away.

He asked if they were hurt, and the girls said no, that they were okay, and they thanked him. He introduced himself as Enrique, and Mia recognized the name. She asked, 'As in Prince Enrique?'

He said yes and then asked if they would like help across the bridge as they were still a bit shaken. He held out his hand to Mia and said, 'Would you like to take my hand, Princess?'

And before Mia could think about her answer, she said, 'Yes, thank you.' Then he helped Roseita off the bridge. She thanked him and then asked Enrique how he knew who the princess was.

'I have a friend who works at the dress shop, and she made the dress that the Princess is wearing.'

Mia was going to tell him the truth, but for some reason, she couldn't. And she didn't know why, but Roseita obviously knew, but she said that her name was Mia and that she was Princess Roseita's maid and best friend.

'Nice to meet both of you,' Enrique said.

Then Roseita said, 'Come on, Princess. It's time to get ready for the ball tonight,' and pulling Mia away.

They said goodbye, and then Mia told Enrique, 'I hope to see you there.'

Back at the palace, in the princess's room, Mia helped the princess get ready for the ball. But Mia looked sad. Princess Roseita asked her what was wrong, and Mia said, 'I'm sad because I lied to the prince. I wanted to tell him the truth, but because I like him, I was scared.' But the princess told her that he deserved to know the truth, and Mia agreed. Roseita said that she could tell him at the ball.

But unknown to them, an uninvited guest was coming to the ball, his name was Carlos, aka the duke. He was an evil man who wanted to marry into the royalty, but he had no success. So he devised a plan in which he would go to the ball in disguise and kidnap the princess.

But then suddenly, Prince Enrique came in. He was the duke's nephew but knew nothing of his foolish plan. He told his uncle about his meeting with the princess. The duke did not know what she looked like. That was part of the problem with the plan, but since his nephew knew what the princess looked like, he thought this would be a good opportunity for him to capture her.

Meanwhile, back at the palace, everyone was getting ready as it was time for the ball and to greet the guests. Everyone was there, including Mia. She was not there as a maid but as a guest. When the ball began, everyone was dancing. Well everyone except Mia and Roseita. Mia was waiting for Enrique, and she was nervous about telling him the truth. But Roseita assured her that it would be okay.

Just then Enrique came in with his uncle. Mia walked over to him, and they said hi to each other. Enrique introduced her to his uncle. Then Mia asked if she could talk to him. He said yes and if anything was wrong. She asked him to meet her where they first met, and he agreed.

But unknown to Mia, someone was following her as she went to meet the prince. When she got there, she heard someone coming. She thought that it was the prince, but it wasn't. It was his uncle, Carlos. He said, 'I have been waiting for you, my bride.' He captured her and took her away.

The prince waited for a while, but Mia never showed up. So he went back to the ball to see if she was with Roseita. When she said no, he explained that she wanted to talk to him about something, but she wasn't there. 'And to make things worse, I can't find my uncle.' Roseita asked him who his uncle was, he said, 'His name is Carlos, but he calls himself the duke.'

Well Roseita went a whiter shade of pale. When Enrique asked what was wrong, she said, 'I'll explain later. Show me where you two were going to meet.'

When they arrived, Roseita saw something on the ground. It was a necklace, and Roseita knew it was hers as it belonged to her mother, and that she would never take it off. 'Enrique, where does your uncle live.' He told her and asked her why. 'I'll explain everything on the way.'

Meanwhile, back at the duke's castle, poor Mia was trapped in a dungeon. She was scared. Then she heard someone come in. It was the duke. 'Hello, Princess. We meet at last.'

At first Mia was puzzled. Then she realized that he thought she was the princess. 'What do you want with the princess?'

'She is going to be my queen.'

'And who are you exactly.'

'I'm Carlos, aka the duke.' A huge gasp came from Mia. 'By the sound of your voice, you must know who I am.'

'Yes, I know who you are. And I know for a fact that the princess will never marry you.' He just laughed and walked out.

As the prince and the princess were on their way to the duke's castle, the prince asked her what was going on. Roseita told him everything—that the duke came to the castle and demanded to marry the princess as he wanted to rule the kingdom. But the king and queen said no, but he said that he would marry her if it was the last thing he'd ever do. The king and queen were scared, but their fear passed as they realized Carlos did not know what the princess looked like. That's why they gave the princess her very first party. Enrique asked, 'How do you know so much about this?'

'It is not my place to say.'

When Roseita and Enrique reached the castle, they went inside and looked for Mia. They came to the dungeon, opened the door, and in they went. They saw Mia, went over to her, and tried to get her out. But before they could, the duke came and found his nephew. The prince asked his uncle, 'Why did you do this?'

The duke looked at him and answered, 'To be king.' Prince Enrique told him to let her go because he loved her.

Then Roseita spoke up. 'This maid is not the princess.'

The duke said. 'That's a lie.'

Roseita said, 'It's the truth. Look at our hands, and you'll know who's who.'

The duke did and then let Mia out. He was going to put Roseita in the dungeon, but before he could, Enrique shoved him in the dungeon instead. The prince locked the door. They were safe.

When they all arrived back at the palace, the king and queen asked where they had been. Roseita and the others explained everything, and they were very happy, and the king and queen told them to go and enjoy the rest of the ball.

And they did. Well, everyone accept Mia. She was sad because she thought that the prince wouldn't talk to her again. But that was not the case. He said, 'Roseita explained everything to me, and I understand. I hoped we can start over again.' Mia was very happy and she said yes.

A few months went by, and Mia and Enrique were more in love than ever. Then they got married, and everyone came, including the king and queen and Roseita. They lived happily ever after.

Well everyone except for the duke. The king and queen banished him from the kingdom.

The Wolf Girl from the Highlands

One stormy night a long time ago, a family was traveling to the Highlands of Scotland to start a new life on a farm. But tragedy struck when their ship was shipwrecked. Sadly, the only survivor was a young girl. She was knocked unconscious, and when she came to, she found herself face-to-face with a wolf.

The young girl was scared. But the wolf meant her no harm. And thanks to her mother instinct and affection, she invited the young girl into the pack, and that's where she stayed.

But then years later, while she was out walking with her pack, the girl spotted a faraway ship. She tried to get a closer look, but the wolf tugged at her clothes as a signal to move on. That night, the girl asked the wolf mother about the visitors. You see, she knew that she was different from her family as she was a very smart and an intelligent girl. When the wolf mother had gotten older, the girl became the protector of the wolf pack. So when she asked about the visitors, it was because she knew that she might need to protect her family.

The next day, while out scouting the Highlands, the girl spotted the strangers; there two men and a girl. As she watched with great caution to see what they were up to, she listened closely. She found out that they were explorers who wanted to learn about wolves and the Highlands.

She was about to go back to report back to the pack, but she lost her footing and fell right in front of the explorers' feet. They were shocked as they had no idea anyone lived there. They asked her who she was, and she told them that she calls herself Wolf Girl. She explained that she was shipwrecked years ago, and the wolves saved her life by adopting her. But she had no memory of who she is or what her name is.

She asked who they were, and they said their names were Angus, Shug, and Caitlyn. Angus started to explain what they were doing there, but she told them that she already knew as she had been watching them. Angus asked her if she could take them to see the wolves as she knew so much about them. She said that she would talk it over with the wolves as it was not just up to her; it was up to the pack. She would meet up with them at the same time tomorrow and give them the pack's decision.

Caitlyn said, 'So you expect us to believe that you speak to the wolves?'

The wolf girl replied, 'Yes I do. I understand them more than any human can ever imagine.' Then she turned and walked away.

She talked it over with the pack, but none of them were sure about meeting the explorers. Wolf Girl suggested that she spend time with them to get more information.

So morning came, and she met the explorers. She told them that the wolves said no, but they were more than welcome to explore and study the Highlands, and she would guide them on their journey. They agreed. Well everyone except Caitlyn, who protested a little. But after Shug talked to her, she calmed down a wee bit.

Angus and Shug were having a great time exploring the Highlands, and they were having fun learning about Wolf Girl, especially Angus as he was starting to really like her. But Catlyn wasn't having any fun. She was more obsessive about going to see the wolves than exploring the Highlands. This made Wolf Girl uneasy.

they eventually stopped to rest for the night. Wolf Girl built a safe fire for them, and they ate some food cooked by Angus and Shug. They all started talking about themselves. Wolf Girl tried to be nice and talk to Caitlyn, but she just got up and walked to where she was sleeping. Shug said, 'Don't worry. She's not been the same since she lost her wee sister years ago.'

Wolf Girl said, 'I am sorry to hear that', but she still didn't understand why Caitlyn wanted to see the wolves so badly. Shug told her that he did not know. Then they went to bed.

In the morning, Angus told Wolf Girl that they would be leaving tomorrow. He asked if she would like to go back with him. She said that she would love to, but, 'I can't leave my family. There's no one to look after them.' And then Angus told her that he loved her.

But before she could say anything, Shug came rushing up to them and said that he couldn't find Caitlyn. He had looked everywhere for her. Wolf Girl said, 'I think I know where she is. She went to see the wolves. We need to find her as she might get hurt.'

So they all went to find her, and they did. She had found the wolf pack. But before she could do anything, Wolf Girl went up to her and asked what she was doing there. Caitlyn said that she wanted to get rid of all the wolves around there. Everyone was shocked, and Wolf Girl asked why. Caitlyn explained, 'After my family returned home after shipwreck, they came without my baby sister.'

'I know this, but what's that got to do with the wolves?' Wolf Girl asked.

'Because my parents believed that she survived. So they took a ship back and searched for her. And what they found was horrible, some ripped clothing. Then they found out that wolves lived there, and they knew what happened.'

Wolf Girl was shocked and puzzled. 'I have not seen anyone else around. And the wolves would not have hurt her as they took care of me. Your sister might still be here. When did your sister disappear?'

Caitlyn said, 'Oh, it was years ago. Her name was Catherine.'

Wolf Girl went into a daze, and Angus asked if she was okay. She said, 'Yes. It is just that I know that name. Maybe I heard it somewhere. Maybe the same place I heard my song.'

'What song?' Caitlyn asked. Wolf Girl sang a few notes, and Caitlin said, 'That's "Speed Bonnie Boat." My Mum used to sing that to me and my wee sister every night before bed.'

Angus and Shug agreed that Wolf Girl was Catherine, Caitlin's sister, and that she survived the shipwreck. The girls looked at each other and decided it was true. They hugged each other and were very happy. They sat down and talked about everything, and that Mum and Dad still hoped that she'd come home.

That night, while everyone slept, Catherine was still awake thinking about what to do. Should she stay in the Highlands, or should she go with Angus and the sister she loved. She couldn't decide, so she went to see the wolf mother for help. She told Catherine, 'Only you can make that decision. But whatever you decide, you're always welcome here.'

'And no matter where I go, you'll always be my mother.' And so with that she walked away. She told Caitlyn and the men that she wanted to go home with them. So when morning came, off they went.

Catherine met her mum and dad, and they were very happy to see her. She was happy to see them, too, but after a few days, she started to miss her old home. She knew that something was wrong. She discussed it with her family, and they agreed to take her to see the wolves.

Everyone got on the ship, including Angus and Shug; Shug was engaged to Caitlyn, and Angus was still in love with Catherine. When they went to the wolf den, Catherine heard the news that her wolf mother had passed on. She was horrified. Now there was no one to look after the pack.

Her family could see how upset she was. Catherine told them what was wrong, and they decided that she should stay and protect her family. They were very proud of her and not to worry. They would visit as often as they could. They told each other they loved them and said goodbye.

At that Angus jumped off the ship and swam across to Catherine. He kissed her and told her that he loved her, and that he would stay with her. She kissed him back and told him that she loved him too. They built a house close to the wolf den, and they all lived happily ever.

A Native American Story

It all started with a dream by a young native American warrior called the Running Bear, that something exciting was about to change his life. Then, he woke up and went for a walk to think about the dream. While he was walking, he came to the ocean bank and he saw something washed up. It was a boat wreck and he saw a strange looking man with a face as white as snow. He was unconscious and hurt, so he took him back to his village to take him to his Father Chief Six Feathers as he was a medicine man and could help him get better. A few days went by and the man started to get well again. When he awoke he found himself in strange surroundings not knowing where he was. He got up and saw that he was well looked after and he wished to thank the people who had saved his life. And then his wish was granted. Running Bear came into the tent and he saw that he was okay. The man introduced himself as James and told Running Bear that he travelled around America as he was a teacher and wanted to learn different cultures and that he knew most of the language well and he also wanted to teach his people of different beliefs and cultures. James asked permission if he could talk to some of his people and learn from them. Running Bear had said that he needed permission from his Father Chief Six Feathers. He also stated that he would need someone to vouch for him and James asked if he would do it. Running Bear agreed so they went to the Chief and asked permission to talk to some of the people and help him understand new cultures. So the Chief thought about it for a moment and then agreed. James was so grateful and excited for this and the next day, he woke up to start his adventure. Then he saw a familiar face. It was Running Bear. James asked how he was and he replied that he was fine and said, "shall we start our day?". James looking confused asked what he meant and Running Bear told him that he might like a guide and a friend with him and James kindly agreed and off they went. A month past, James and Running Bear was learning so much but they were also learning something new that would change both their lives. They both realised that they had feelings for each other. Running Bear was happy as he understood what his dream was telling him. On the other hand, James was scared as he loved Running Bear but he knew that his people might not accept his love for another man as he came from another country England and his culture was very different from the native Americans'. So he decided to confide to the Chief and ask him for advice about what he should do as they became quite close. He explained to Chief Six Feathers that his people did not know that he was in love with a man. When they had written them, he did not mention it. He also said that if he went back home he could not leave Running Bear as he loved him but he did not know if Running Bear felt the same way. The Chief told him that he should be talking to Running Bear and see what he thinks so that's what James did. It turned out that Running Bear felt the exact same way. Then a sense of relief came over James, but the worry was still there and Running Bear saw that and he lean into James and kissed him. Then that night in Running Bears tipi as he lay sleeping, he had another dream about something troubling. The next morning as he went to go and tell James, just before he could tell him, the native Americans told them that some more people has come. It was James' family and friends. He asked how they got here. They had told him they got there by ship and they thought that they would see if he was ready to come home as it did not say in the letter. Trying to change the subject, he asked permission from the Chief if they could bed down for the night and have some food as the night grew. James was trying to avoid the subject of going home instead all he talked about was his journey and how much he learned and how they saved him from harm when his boat got wrecked. As he saw Running Bear walk away, he excused himself and went with him into the forest. He asked him what was wrong and he told James about his dream that something terrible was going to happen. James was trying to comfort him but they both knew what the trouble was. James assured him that everything will work out. They'll make them see that it's okay to be different and be in love with whoever they want man or woman. And with that, they shared other kiss. Unknown to them they were being watched and listened to by one of James' friends and he ran to tell his family and the others what he saw. He did not like the native Americans to begin with as he wanted their land so he saw this as an opportunity to try and get it. He had twisted it to make it that Running Bear had casted a spell on him and it was the natives' fault. Enraged by this, they wanted to put a stop to this. So they decided to capture Running Bear and ran out the native Americans. That night when everyone was sleeping, James' family hatched their evil plan and they captured Running Bear and his tribe. They put James in a cage he was trying to get some answers but no one was giving him any. As luck would have it, one of the natives got away. Her name was Water Lily and she managed to find James and helped him escape. He had asked her what happened and she explained everything and that they were going to get rid of Running Bear. He hurried to where they were as Water Lily told him. And he saw Running Bear so he ran as fast as he could and before anyone knew it he threw himself into Running Bear's arms. He told them to stop and his family told him to step back. He told them that he can't as he loved him and that they have been lied to. He was not put under any evil spell the only spell he was under is love. They turned to the man who had said this and they asked him to explain himself. When he had no answer, he ran away because he knew that he could not win. His family turned to James and the tribe and they had the look of shame on their faces. They apologised but James had told them that they had nothing to be sorry for as they were just trying to protect him. He asked his family if they could forgive him as he did not tell them about Running Bear. They said, "of course" and they said from what they could see he was a very nice boy and they are happy to accept him. James had also decided to stay with Running Bear as a teacher for the native Americans so he saw his family off to the ship to say goodbye and come and visit soon. And they all lived happily ever after.

The End

Akcheta (The Fighter)

Once upon a time in America when the country belonged to the natives, there lived a tribe of people. They lived very well in their native cultures but through time some new people came to their country and made some of their land their own. They called them settlers, but that's not what this story is about. This happened a few years after when another ship of settlers came across the river. They were not like any other. They did not want to trade or keep the peace. They were pirates and the captain decide to settle on the land. When the American Chief heard of this, he decided to confront him and he said that the only way he would be at peace was if the Chief would sell one of his daughters to him to be his wife. He had three days to do this or there will be trouble. So he went back to his village scarred and heartbroken. He told his only daughter, her name was Akcheta and she said that she would go but not to worry as she had a plan and she kissed him and off she went. On arrival, the pirate saw how outstandingly beautiful she was, but when he approached her, she started to transform into a wolf. She was able to do this as she was a shapeshifter. When the pirate saw this, he ran so scared that he got on his ship and went away. When the princess tried to shape back, she couldn't. Confused and worried, the only thing she could do was to go back to the village and try to speak to her father. When she got there, her father found it odd to find a wolf in the village. When he looked into the wolf's eyes, he realized that it was his daughter. All the Wolf could do was howl and that was a sign of sadness and her father knew that something went wrong. Now her father had to try and reverse the spell but he didn't know much about magic. He only knew how to temporally reverse it. You see the daughter learned magic from her mother but passed on before she could teach them anymore. So the father transformed her back and explained that she will only turn human when the night sets, but there was another way to break it if she traveled to the mountains were the spirits are and she'll be turned back. But her father did not dare her to go alone and she also did not know the way so her father arranged an escort for her. A young brave warrior, his name was Golden Eagle. She packed her food, kissed her father and off they went to start the journey. On the way there she had asked Golden Eagle how long and far the mountain is and he replied "it would take a week to get there". Then Akcheta got worried as Golden Eagle did not know about her shapeshifting into a wolf. A few hours past and they decided to have a rest and finally

Golden Eagle asked her why does she want to talk to the spirits on the mountains. After a little time of thinking on how to tell him, she finally explained what happened to her and that she had to transform back or maybe at least try and control it so if danger does come across again, I can shift without the fear of never shifting back. After talking, they set up the camp and then all of a sudden night had fallen and Akcheta turned into a wolf, but Golden Eagle was not scared so they decided to get sleep because they have a big day tomorrow. A funny thing about time, it passes quickly. A week was there and the mountain was just round the corner and she couldn't believe that they had made it. As soon as he reached the mountain, the spirits appeared. They knew why Akcheta was there and then her mother appeared and told her that she was the only one that had the power to control it. As long as she is scared and angry, she will continue to have these feelings she will not be able to control the shape shifting. Then the spirit went away. She understood what to do. She had to practice to control it. So the only thing that she could do is get help from the medicine man called Silver Wolfe. She was worried as she felt it might not work, but Golden Eagle assured her that it will because she is kind sweet and determined and with that he gave her a gentle kiss. She looked at him and gave him a sweet smile and kissed him back, decided to be on their way to go back home to see her father. As they reached home to the village she explained everything to her father and they made arrangements to go and see Silver Wolfe. As they approached the outskirts of the village they saw Silver Wolfe and approached him. The chief went up to him and introduced himself and started to tell him what had happened with his daughter, but Silver Wolfe already new of Akcheta's fate. They looked puzzled so Silver Wolfe sat them down and started to explain that a girl similar to her was the same and the girl was Akcheta's mother. This was long before she had met her father and the only way that he could help was for her to listen to her heart and believe in herself and love is also a very powerful tool. Silver Wolfe told the same thing to Akcheta and she realized that. Silver Wolfe had said that she could control it with the help of her people and loved ones. They went home and in time she had learned to control it and had no worries about shape shifting back and forth. She also had gotten married to Golden Eagle and they all lived happily ever after.

The End

Printed in the United States
by Baker & Taylor Publisher Services